IF YOU WERE A TIGER CUB

For Sebby and Winnie

IF YOU WERE A TIGER CUB

Stephen Alter

Illustrations by

Mohit Suneja

ALEPH

ALEPH BOOK COMPANY
An independent publishing firm
promoted by ***Rupa Publications India***

First published in India in 2024
by Aleph Book Company
7/16 Ansari Road, Daryaganj
New Delhi 110 002

This is a work of fiction. Names, characters, places, and incidents are either the product of the authors' imagination or are used fictitiously and any resemblance to any actual persons, living or dead, events, or locales is entirely coincidental.

ISBN: 978-81-974969-5-0

1 3 5 7 9 10 8 6 4 2

Printed in India

IF YOU WERE A TIGER CUB

If you were a tiger cub, you'd wake up early in the morning and yawn, as if you were going to swallow the sky. Before the sun appears above the treetops, you would get up and follow your mother, and your two brothers, to a still pool of clear water, where a stream from the hills collects in a sandy hollow surrounded by big rocks. You'd drink as much water as your tummy can hold and then flop down on the sand to watch a red dragonfly skimming over the pool.

If you were a tiger cub, you'd wrestle with your brothers at the water's edge. Though they are bigger and stronger than you and like to bully their sister, you'd know how to bite their tails with your sharp little teeth. Yelping, they'd run to your mother for protection while you'd snarl at them, as if to say, 'Boys, don't mess with me. I'm your little sister but I'll never let you beat me at any game.'

And then, as if to prove that you are braver than them, you'd jump into the water and swim across to the other side of the pool and climb onto the biggest rock. If you were a tiger cub, you'd stand on top of the rock like the queen of the jungle, daring your brothers to swim across too. Neither of them likes to get

wet and one of them can't swim, so instead of following you into the water, they'd circle around the pool and jump over the stream, then try to climb onto your rock.

Being a tiger cub, you'd nip at their ears and growl until they give up. Then you'd leap off the rock and into the pool, splashing across to your mother who is lying in the shade of a banyan tree. Shaking the water from your coat, you'd curl up beside her, in the best spot of all, next to the soft fur on her belly, against the curve of her hind leg, where your brothers like to lie together, just as they did when they were babies.

A hornbill is eating figs in the banyan tree above you, dropping some of them on your head. If you were a tiger cub, you'd glare at the bird with your big tiger eyes and then get up and climb onto one of the hanging roots on the banyan, grabbing it with both paws

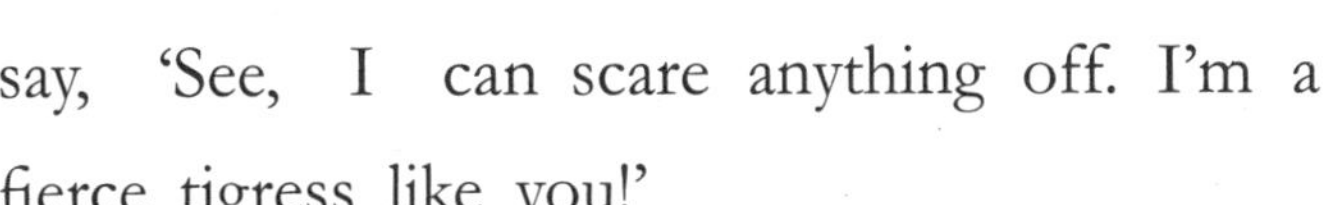

and swinging back and forth. When the hornbill flies away, you'd look at your mother as if to say, 'See, I can scare anything off. I'm a fierce tigress like you!'

If you were a tiger cub, waiting for your two dumb brothers to make up their minds which way to circle back around the pool, you'd see a python lying in the shallows, with only its head sticking out of the water. Creeping forward, you'd wade into the pool and swat the snake's tail, so that it goes slithering out, just as your brothers come bounding across. Seeing the python, they'd both trip over each other and tumble backwards with fright, as the snake slides away into the shadows.

Your two brothers are still whimpering and

shaking with fear, so you'd go across and lick their faces to calm them down. After all, what's a little sister good for except to comfort her big brothers when they get scared? If you were a tiger cub, you'd let your brothers know that there's nothing to be afraid of, but when they turn their backs and head towards your mother, you'd hiss through your teeth, making a sound just like a python. Your brothers would both jump in the air and scramble to safety, while you wave your tail at them as if it were a snake.

Later on, when your mother goes hunting, you'd lead the way and sniff the air to see if there is anything good to eat, maybe a deer or a wild boar. If you were a tiger cub, you'd creep through the jungle without making a sound. Your mother would have taught you how to listen for noises in the forest that signal who else is nearby. You'd hear birds calling in the trees overhead, or the rustle of

dry leaves on the ground as a leopard moves out of your path, or the blustery snort of an elephant hidden behind a clump of bamboo. None of these are animals you'd want to eat. But, suddenly, you'd hear a sound that makes you stop!

If you were a tiger cub, you'd know exactly what it is… the alarm call of a sambar deer! It's a sharp, honking cry, warning other animals in the jungle that a tigress and her three cubs

are prowling about. You'd stand very still, as your mother moves forward through the shadows and crouches behind a bush covered with yellow flowers. The sambar is very close and each time the deer calls, the sound would make you shiver with excitement. Behind you, your brothers would be standing side by side, waiting impatiently for your mother to catch the deer. The only thing that moves is a feathery seed that drifts down from a silk cotton tree overhead. As it floats by one of your brothers, he'd sniff at it and the seed would go up his nose.

'Aaatchoo!'

The sambar races away through the forest and all of the other animals nearby take flight. Your mother would glance over her shoulder with an impatient frown and if you were a tiger cub, you'd give your brother the same disapproving look, for ruining the hunt. Of course, he would try to pretend it wasn't him that sneezed and blame it on you, though the feathered seed is still sticking out of his nose and you'd brush it away with your paw. His stomach growls hungrily and your stomach would growl back at him, as if to say, 'Come on. Can't you do anything right?'

If you were a tiger cub, your mother would take you and your two brothers to a secret cave at the foot of a cliff and leave you there, while she goes off to hunt on her own. She wouldn't have to say anything, but you'd know that this is a place where you will be safe, while she is away. You'd also know, without being told, that you mustn't wander off on your own and that when she comes back, your mother will have found something to eat. Until then, you and your brothers must wait and not make a sound.

Of course, once your mother slips away into the forest, your brothers begin to fidget and fuss. One of them might nudge you with his nose, trying to get you to move to the back of the cave while the other would push you aside with his paws, though there's plenty of room for all three of you. Getting up, you'd slink away to the darkest corner of the cave and climb onto a high ledge, then spring into the air to scare the bats that are hanging from the ceiling. All of them would fly off together, swooping down over your brothers' heads. Being a brave little tigress, you wouldn't be afraid of bats, but your two brothers will panic and scramble out of the cave, diving under bushes and vines to escape.

If you were a tiger cub, you'd stretch out comfortably at the mouth of the cave with a little tiger smile on your lips as you watch your brothers peeking out nervously from beneath

the leaves to make sure nothing is flying about. You might even lift one paw and wave at them, as if to say, 'Hi there, boys. What are you hiding from?' A little while later, they'd both come crawling back to the cave but let you have as much space as you want. Now that you're comfortable, you'd put your chin on your paws and fall asleep.

Being a tiger cub, you'd dream of becoming a full-grown tigress one day, queen of the jungle. As you walk through a palace of trees, all of the birds in the branches overhead would sing your praises, and the animals would bow down before you. Everyone in the jungle will obey your commands and whenever you roar, even the elephants would tremble with fear. Nobody dares to challenge you, not even your brothers. They'd both do whatever they were told, bringing you food whenever you are hungry and letting you rest on the softest moss while fanning you with their tails to chase away flies.

But suddenly, you'd wake up out of your dreams and realize that something is wrong. Your brothers aren't here in the cave and when you look around, they are nowhere in sight. Being the only tiger cub with any brains, you'd know that the two of them must have wandered off while you were asleep, even though you're not supposed to leave this spot. Now, what should you do? With an impatient sigh, you'd get to your feet and sniff the ground to see which way they've gone. It's easy to follow their scent as you stalk through the jungle. They can't be too far away.

But then, if you were a tiger cub, you'd smell something that would make the hairs on your back quiver and stand on end. It's a strong, stinky smell, which you'd recognize right away. At that same moment, you would

hear the angry scream of a sloth bear, followed by two yowling cries for help and you'd know that your brothers are in trouble. Hurrying through a thicket of ferns and jumping over a dead log, you'd come to a clearing where the shaggy bear is standing next to a termite castle, which he was about to tear down with his sharp claws. Termites are his favourite food and your brothers have disturbed him, just as he was about to have lunch.

Cowering behind a tree, your brothers are trying to hide. If you were a tiger cub, you'd keep out of sight in the bushes and roar, as loud as you can. But the sound you'd make wouldn't frighten the bear. He'd turn around and scream, baring his teeth and waving his long, sharp claws. Looking anxiously about, you'd spot a hollow tree. Then, knowing exactly what to do, you'd put your mouth next to a hole in the trunk and when you roar again, the sound would echo up through the hollow tree and out the top. This time the roar is even louder than your mother's, as deep and frightening as thunder. Hearing the roar, the bear would think a giant tiger is nearby so he'd turn around and run away, as fast as a sloth bear can run.

Once the danger is gone, your brothers would come swaggering out from behind the tree, as if they're the ones who scared off the bear. Looking at you with ungrateful scowls, they would act as if they'd conquered the termite castle. Joining the two heroes and rubbing your cheeks against their necks while purring softly, you'd reach out with one paw and knock off the top of the termite castle. All at once, swarms of white ants would come streaming out of the broken mud walls and crawl up your brothers' legs. Both of them would start dancing about, making helpless, terrified squeaks. With their tails between their legs, they'd both go racing back to the cave.

If you were a tiger cub, you'd follow your brothers but then hide in the grass to watch what they do next. Licking their paws and shaking themselves to get rid of the last termites crawling through their fur, they'd lie down without looking at each other, as if they don't want to admit that they were afraid of teeny-tiny ants. Neither of them would seem to miss you or wonder where you are. All they ever think about is themselves. But being a brave little tigress, you wouldn't care, because you'd know you're smarter than them.

Just then, your mother would return from the hunt, with a big juicy boar that she'd drop on the ground in front of the cave. Seeing that lunch is here, your two brothers would jump down and rush at the boar without any manners. Your mother would growl at them and make them back off. Being a well-behaved tiger cub, you'd come out of hiding and wait until your mother takes the first bite. Then you'd join her and eat your fill, while your brothers have to wait and watch impatiently, until your mother finally gives them permission to feed.

After everyone has eaten as much as they can, you'd all lie down in the cave. Your mother, who is tired from hunting, would be the first to fall asleep. So would your brothers because their stomachs are full. But you wouldn't be sleepy because earlier today, you had a nap. Being a tiger cub, you'd listen for sounds in the forest and recognize the faraway call of a peacock or the grunt of a gaur. Then somewhere nearby, you'd hear someone singing, a soft, sad song. This sound is different from anything you've ever heard before and you'd know that it isn't a bird.

If you were a tiger cub, your curiosity would make you get up and slip out of the cave on your own. Stepping silently through the dead leaves on the forest floor, you'd make your way towards the sound. Coming to a tangled jumble of bushes, you'd lie down on your belly and peer through the curtain of leaves. On the other side of the bushes is a clearing, with beams of sunlight streaming through the high branches. In the middle of the clearing is an animal you've never seen before. She is standing on her hind legs, with her arms in the air. Her long, black hair is plaited in a neat braid. While gathering dry sticks in the forest, she is singing softly to herself in a voice that sounds familiar.

Lying as still as a caterpillar in its cocoon, you'd watch this strange creature as she moves about under the trees, collecting dead branches and twigs, which she piles together in a heap on the ground. Why is she doing this? you'd wonder. After circling around the clearing, she comes toward the bush where you're hiding. For a moment, you'd think that maybe you should get up and slip quietly away, but she is looking right at you. If you move, this strange creature would certainly see you. So, you'd hold your breath, without twitching an ear or a whisker, as she leans down in front of the bush and reaches out to pick up a dry piece of wood. One end of it is sticking out of the bush while the other end is pressed under

your forepaw. As she tries to pull it free, her hand brushes the leaves aside and she sees you crouched under the bush, staring at her. All at once, the singing stops.

Now, if you were a tiger cub, what would you do?

Would you growl and make a fierce face, showing your sharp teeth? Would you get to your feet and leap out of the bush to prove how bold and strong you are? Would you scare this animal with a loud roar and chase her away?

If you were a tiger cub, what do you think you would do?

Would you turn tail and run? Would you escape through the forest and never look back? Would you be so scared that you'd race to your cave and hide behind your big brothers, even if you know they would never protect you?